MEET THE COMMUNITY HELPERS!

A DAY WITH A LIBRARIAN

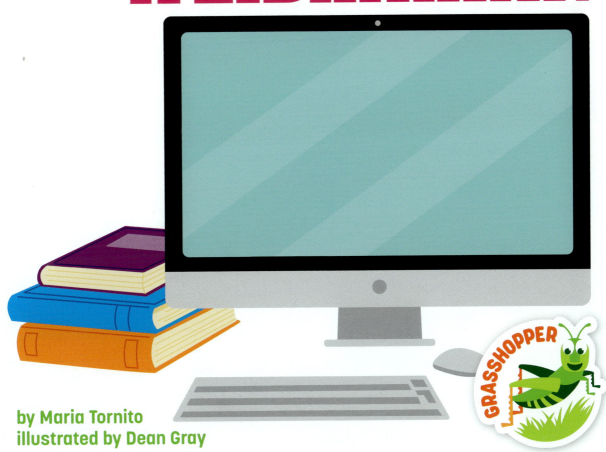

by Maria Tornito
illustrated by Dean Gray

GRASSHOPPER

Tools for Parents & Teachers

Grasshopper Books enhance imagination and introduce the earliest readers to fiction with fun storylines and illustrations. The easy-to-read text supports early reading experiences with repetitive sentence patterns and sight words.

Before Reading

- Discuss the cover illustration. What do they see?

- Look at the picture glossary together. Discuss the words.

Read the Book

- Read the book to the child, or have him or her read independently.

- "Walk" through the book and look at the illustrations. Who is the main character? What is happening in the story?

After Reading

- Prompt the child to think more. Ask: Have you ever met a librarian? Would you like to?

Grasshopper Books are published by Jump!
5357 Penn Avenue South
Minneapolis, MN 55419
www.jumplibrary.com

Library of Congress Cataloging-in-Publication Data

Names: Tornito, Maria, author. | Gray, Dean, illustrator.
Title: A day with a librarian / by Maria Tornito; illustrated by Dean Gray.
Description: Minneapolis, MN: Jump!, Inc., [2022]
Series: Meet the community helpers!
Includes reading tips and supplementary back matter.
Audience: Ages 5–8.
Identifiers: LCCN 2021001582 (print)
LCCN 2021001583 (ebook)
ISBN 9781636902166 (hardcover)
ISBN 9781636902173 (paperback)
ISBN 9781636902180 (ebook)
Subjects: LCSH: Readers (Primary)
Librarians–Juvenile fiction.
Classification: LCC PE1119.2 .T6288 2022 (print)
LCC PE1119.2 (ebook) | DDC 428.6/2–dc23
LC record available at https://lccn.loc.gov/2021001582
LC ebook record available at https://lccn.loc.gov/2021001583

Editor: Eliza Leahy
Direction and Layout: Anna Peterson
Illustrator: Dean Gray

Printed in the United States of America at Corporate Graphics in North Mankato, Minnesota.

Table of Contents

Checking Out Books

It is story time at the library.

The librarian, Mr. Fisher, reads a book about lions.

"Do you have other animal books, Mr. Fisher?" asks Carlos.

"Yes! Follow me," Mr. Fisher says.

"Here are some you might like," says Mr. Fisher.

"I'll take them!" Carlos says.

Mr. Fisher leads Carlos to another shelf.

Carlos picks out books about sharks.

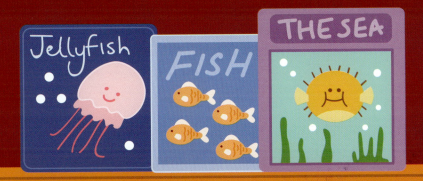

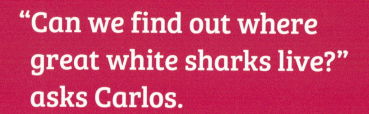

"Can we find out where great white sharks live?" asks Carlos.

"We sure can!" says Mr. Fisher. "This is the reference section. Encyclopedias have lots of information."

"You can also find information online," Mr. Fisher says.

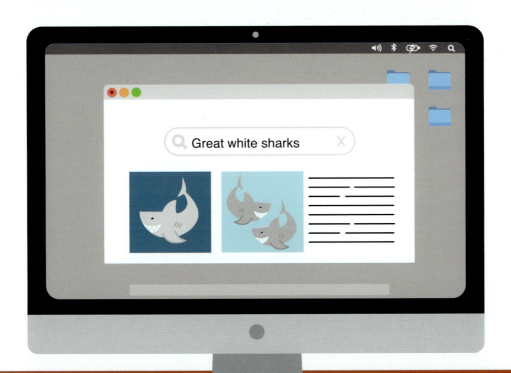

Great white sharks

"You can look up a topic," says Mr. Fisher.

Carlos types in the search bar.
Lots of information comes up!

"What is that librarian doing?" Carlos asks.

"She is putting books back on their shelves. That's what we do with them after they're returned," says Mr. Fisher.

They walk by the front desk.

"Can I check these books out?" asks Carlos.

"Of course! Do you have your library card?" Mr. Fisher asks.

"Yep!" says Carlos.

BOOK RETURNS

17

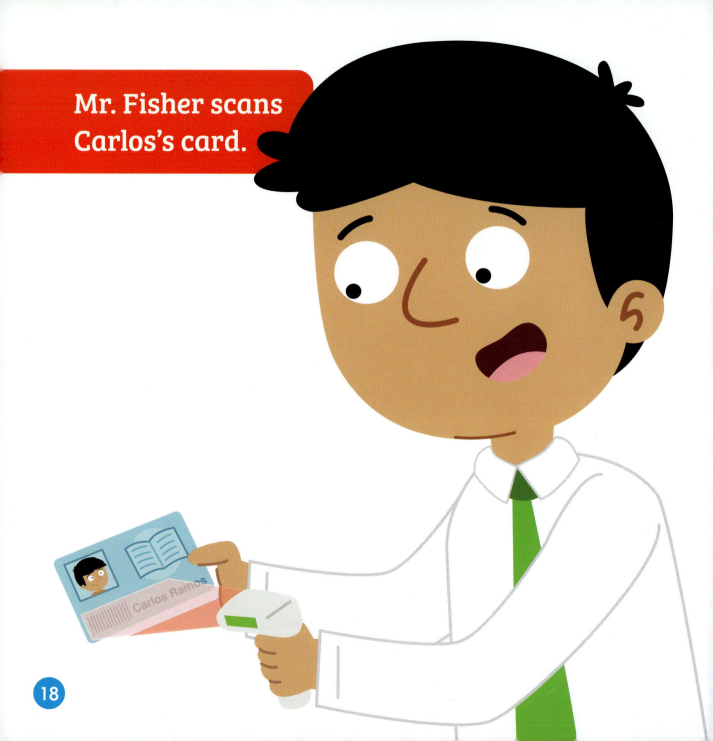

Mr. Fisher scans Carlos's card.

BOOK RETURNS

"These books are due in three weeks," says Mr. Fisher. "You can put them in this slot when you bring them back."

"I will return them
on time," Carlos says.
"Thanks, Mr. Fisher.
See you soon!"

"Happy reading!"
Mr. Fisher says.

Quiz Time!

What is one thing Mr. Fisher doesn't show Carlos in the library?

A. the printer   **B.** the reference section
C. the book return slot   **D.** the front desk

Library Resources

These are some of the resources Carlos and Mr. Fisher use in the story. Can you point to them in the book?

computer

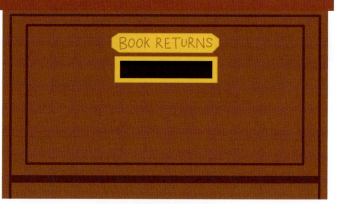

book return slot

encyclopedias

library card

Picture Glossary

encyclopedias
Books or sets of books with very detailed information.

information
Facts or knowledge that you learn from exploring, listening, or reading.

reference
Something that leads a reader to another source of information.

scans
Moves a beam of light over something to transmit an image.

shelf
A length of wood or other hard material that is used for holding or storing objects.

topic
The subject of a discussion, study, lesson, speech, or piece of writing.

Index

To Learn More

Finding more information is as easy as 1, 2, 3.

❶ Go to www.factsurfer.com

❷ Enter "**adaywithalibrarian**" into the search box.

❸ Choose your book to see a list of websites.